DISCARD

TOUCANS, TOO

TOUCANS, TOO

Bethanie Deeney Murguia

little bee books

For Kendall

🐝 little bee books

An imprint of Bonnier Publishing USA | 251 Park Avenue South, New York, NY 10010
Copyright © 2017 by Bethanie Deeney Murguia | All rights reserved, including the right of reproduction in whole
or in part in any form. LITTLE BEE BOOKS is a trademark of Bonnier Publishing USA, and associated colophon
is a trademark of Bonnier Publishing USA.
Manufactured in China   LEO 1116
First Edition   10 9 8 7 6 5 4 3 2 1
Library of Congress Cataloging-in-Publication Data is available upon request.
ISBN 978-1-4998-0421-8
littlebeebooks.com   bonnierpublishingusa.com

Cockatoo.

Cockatoo, too.

One can. Two cans.

Toucans?

Toucans, too!

Toucan stew???!

Toucan? Toucan?

Oooooooooooooh, stew!

Toucan canoe!

New two-can stew!

One canoe. Stew canoe!

Can gnu? Can gnu?

Gnu cockatoo toucan stew-can canoe.

Cuckoos, too!